Many happy tea parties!

Babette Donaldson

Emma Lea's First Tea Party

Written by Babette Donaldson • Illustrated by Jerianne Van Dijk

Published by Blue Gate Books, Nevada City, California

Requests for permission to make copies of any part of the work should be mailed to:
Permissions Department
Blue Gate Books
P.O. Box 2137
Nevada City, CA 95959
(530) 478-0365

Summary: Emma Lea is finally old enough to join her mother and aunts for
her grandmother's annual birthday tea party.

ISBN 978-0-9792612-0-6

[1. Juvenile Fiction 2. Tea 3. Family Tea Party 4. Birthday Party]

Library of Congress Control Number: 2007900903

Printed in China

Blue Gate Books
P.O. Box 2137
Nevada City, CA 95959

Design and computer production by Patty Arnold
Menagerie Design and Publishing www.menageriedesign.net

Dedicated to:

Chris & Jeff – Fritz & John

Mama was helping Emma Lea get ready for Grammy's special birthday tea party. Emma Lea was finally old enough to go with her mother and her three aunts. Grammy started the tradition when Mama and her sisters were old enough to sit at the big table in the dining room and sip from the special china cups without spilling tea on the lace tablecloth.

"I want to look like a big girl for Grammy," Emma Lea told Mama. She sat as still as she could while Mama combed the snaggles out of her hair and wove shiny satin ribbons into her braids.

"You are a big girl." Mama smiled. "Just look at you."

Emma Lea practiced the song she would sing for Grammy as Mama pinned the braids around her head like a crown. She watched in the mirror. She felt like she was being changed into a princess in her beautiful party dress.

Emma Lea could see her father in the mirror, watching from the open door. "You look Love-A-Lea." He came in and kissed her on the cheek. "Tell Grammy Happy Birthday for me." He kissed Mama too. "I wish I could join you."

"Whoever heard of boys at tea parties?" Emma Lea teased. But she secretly wished the same thing.

"You'd look silly in one of Grammy's party hats." Mama teased him too.

He took Mama's straw sunbonnet from the coat rack and put it sideways on his head. He pretended he was wearing a big, wide skirt, swishing it around like he was dancing. "I would use my very best manners and bring a really, really big present."

"Grammy doesn't want presents from a store," Mama explained. "She wants us to sing songs and read poems and tell the stories we've written that make us all laugh and dream."

"You've written an especially good story this year," Daddy told Mama.

"And she gives us the presents," Emma Lea added. "She gives everyone a teacup." Emma Lea pretended to drink from an imaginary cup with her head tipped back and her little finger pointed in the air.

"So we can give parties for our own daughters and friends," Mama said.

"I'll fix tea for you too, Daddy." She hugged her father goodbye.

When they got to Grammy's house, Emma Lea helped Mama carry in their trays. One was stacked with fancy sandwiches. The other tray was filled with tiny tea cookies.

"We're here." Emma Lea called loudly above the chatter inside. "Happy Birthday!"

Everyone wore special outfits and one of Grammy's fancy hats.

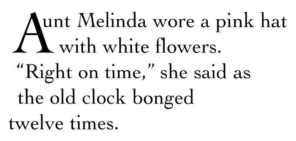

Aunt Melinda wore a pink hat
with white flowers.
"Right on time," she said as
the old clock bonged
twelve times.

Aunt Miriam wore a purple
hat with a soft, velvet
ribbon tied in a bow.
"Come here, my
beautiful, little niece."
Aunt Miriam gave her such
a big, mother-bear hug;
it nearly knocked the
purple hat off her head.

"See, I'm not so little
anymore, Auntie Mim."
Emma Lea replied.

Grammy finished pinning a yellow hat with orange flowers on Aunt Meg's head as she said, "Look at you, Emma Lea. You've grown another inch."

She pinned a sparkling tiara into Emma Lea's braids. Now Emma Lea really felt like a princess.

"Welcome to your first real tea party."

The big table in the dining room was covered with a lace tablecloth. The matching napkins were rolled into silver rings. A centerpiece of fresh-cut garden flowers filled the room with the sparkling smell of spring.

Aunt Melinda lit the candles. Aunt Miriam poured hot tea into the silver teapot and set it out with a matching sugar bowl and cream pitcher. Aunt Meg cut thin wedges of the spinach quiche and arranged them on a gold-rimmed china platter.

Mama made space for the tray of sandwiches on the table with the bowl of fruit, the raspberry scones, lemon cream, homemade candies, shortbread cookies and the tiny, decorated cakes. As soon as her hands were empty, Grammy gave Mama a beautiful green hat with dark trim and bright turquoise peacock feathers.

Grammy's best china plates and her favorite antique teacups were set at each place around the table. She told a story about each one. "This was my great-grandmother's. She brought it with her from the old country."

As Emma Lea listened, she walked around the table looking at each fragile cup and saucer. She counted five places set at the big table. Something was wrong. She counted the cups again while Grammy went to the kitchen for one last thing.

Emma Lea started to tell Mama about the cups when Grammy came out from the kitchen with a plastic tray. She set it on a small table in the corner of the dining room close to the kitchen door. It was the table where Emma Lea sat with her younger cousins at family gatherings and holiday dinners while the grownups crowded around the big table.

"I fixed some special things for you to do so you won't be bored," Grammy said.

The tray was filled with sticker books, glitter paper and gel pens; special art supplies that would delight Emma Lea on any other day. But sitting at a separate table like a little girl wasn't what she wanted to do today.

Aunt Meg brought out a regular teacup and saucer from the kitchen filled with Emma Lea's favorite tea. It was Grammy's special blend - a pink, fruity tea she made for the children. It was not what Emma Lea wanted today.

On this special day she wanted to drink the Oolong tea Grammy would pour from the big, silver pot. It was a rare tea from China. Aunt Miriam described the remote plantation where the tea was grown and how the women of a small village picked it by hand.

Emma Lea was quiet, as the talk at the big table grew louder.

Mama filled a plate with Emma Lea's favorite treats. She knelt beside her daughter's chair and whispered, "It's not what we thought it would be." She tucked a stray bit of hair back into Emma Lea's pretty braids. "But let's do this Grammy's way."

Emma Lea nodded to her mother with tight lips to hold her crying inside.

"It's very grown-up not to show Grammy how disappointed you are."

After Mama returned to her place at the big table, Emma Lea slipped quietly into the kitchen and out the back door. She headed for the old tree swing next to Grampop's workshop.

Grampop saw Emma Lea on the swing and came out to talk with her. "Didn't you like the tea party?"

Emma Lea couldn't hold the tears back. Grampop knelt down on the grass so he could look straight into her eyes.

"There, there, little one." He tried to comfort her.

"I'm not little anymore," Emma Lea snapped back. She didn't mean to sound so angry. She wished she could bite the words back into her mouth. But it was too late. Grampop waited patiently for her to explain. "Grammy put me at the baby table."

"Oh, I see."

Emma Lea could see his gentle eyes through the blur of tears. He did understand.

Grampop held out his strong hand. "Would you like to have tea with me?"

Emma Lea nodded and slipped her small hand into his. Grampop's workshop was filled with shelves full of the cups, teapots, platters and bowls he made from clay. On top of his kiln—the big oven where he was baking a new batch of clay pots—was his sturdy, handmade teapot.

He chose one of the big mugs for her. They were different from Grammy's delicate teacup collection, but each one had a story.

"My friends and I made these when we were in college. I keep them to remember those days. No one who saw my first pieces thought I would become an artist and sell my work."

He let Emma Lea hold the dusty teapot with a crooked handle and a lopsided lid. It made her laugh. Pretty soon she was able to talk about Grammy's tea party without sniffing.

Grampop added milk and honey to Emma Lea's tea. Even with the milk, it was still hot and strong—dark brown and musty smelling.

"Now," he asked her, "tell me what happened."

Grammy came to the door. She waited out-of-sight, listening. They didn't know she was there.

"She didn't mean to hurt your feelings," Grampop explained.

"I know." Emma Lea was already feeling better.

"It's not about being dressed up and eating fancy food at the big table." Grampop made his voice low and serious. He took her hand in his big rough one. "It's about celebrating an important day, just the way Grammy likes it. The tea parties are special. Something she did with her own mother and grandmother. Something she wants to continue in our family."

There was a little bit of sadness in Grampop's voice as he explained how he wished he could go to the birthday tea parties too. Emma Lea understood.

So did Grammy.

"Daddy wanted to come too," Emma Lea told Grampop. "Tea parties should be for everyone. Not just for grown-up ladies."

Emma Lea watched Grampop smile as he warmed his hands around his tea mug. She guessed he was imagining himself at Grammy's birthday party.

"Why don't you tell Grammy how you feel?" she asked. "Why don't you?" Grampop answered.

Grammy couldn't wait outside the door any longer. "What are you two doing out here?"

They were so startled, they almost spilled their tea.

"Come inside, both of you." She took Grampop's heavy teapot from the top of the kiln and carried it inside.

"Poppa's come to tea," Aunt Melinda cheered.

"And we're all sitting at the big table," Grammy said.

Mama set two more places at the table. "Would you sit beside me, Emma Lea?"

Just then, Emma Lea remembered, "Grammy, Daddy wanted me to tell you Happy Birthday from him. He wished he could be here too."

"Next year, everyone comes to my birthday." She winked at Emma Lea. "That's what birthdays and tea parties are all about." She leaned close to Emma Lea's ear and whispered, "Thank you."

"I learned a special song for you." Emma Lea stood straight and tall and sang with extra sparkle in her voice. It was a familiar tune but Daddy had helped her write new lyrics, just for this special day.

Then Aunt Meg recited a poem she wrote.

Aunt Melinda and Aunt Miriam played a flute duet.

Mama read her new story.

Grampop was the last one. He described the first time he saw Grammy. They were children in the same school. They had been together for a very long time. It wasn't a new story but it still made everyone cry.

This time, Emma Lea didn't try to hide her tears. She let the happy drops squeeze from the corner of her eyes as she imagined Grampop and Grammy as children.

"You should have told me you wanted to come to tea," Grammy pretended to scold Grampop.

"Who ever heard of boys at tea parties?" Grampop made a silly face.

Grammy brought out gift boxes - four small ones and one larger one. The small ones were the teacups for Mama and her sisters. The large one was for Emma Lea.

"A teapot!" Emma Lea was so excited and bouncy, she almost knocked her tiara loose. "A real, grown-up sized teapot." She held it up so they could all see.

"Now everyone can come to tea with me!"

The Illustrations are original watercolor
paintings by Jerianne Van Dijk.

AUTHOR

BABETTE DONALDSON is the author and creator of the Emma Lea stories. She has a BA in Creative Writing and a BFA in Ceramic Art from San Francisco State University and received her tea certification from the Specialty Tea Institute, the education division of The Tea Council of the United States. She is currently the director of Tea Suite, a non-profit organization supporting art education.

ILLUSTRATOR

JERIANNE VAN DIJK—An artist for over 30 years, Jerianne Van Dijk's award-winning illustrations have graced calendars, greeting cards, product labels, posters and books. She is proficient in various media and is as happy doing botanicals as goofy whimsical things to make you think. Jerianne began working as a graphic designer for an array of advertising agencies, newspapers, and printing companies. She particularly enjoys freelance illustration as one of her many specialties. Residing in Northern California as a watercolor instructor, fine artist and illustrator Jerianne enjoys the work her gift affords her. For more about her work visit www.jerianne.net

DESIGNER

PATTY ARNOLD is the owner of *Menagerie Design and Publishing*—a small company specializing in book production. She has a BFA in sculpture and printmaking, a BS in Graphic Communications and an MFA in Photography and Digital Imaging. She also teaches Graphic Design, Typography and Digital Arts at the local community college and is an exhibiting photographer. You can view her fine art at www.pattyarnold.com and her design projects at www.menageriedesign.net.

Emma Lea's Magic Teapot
Emma Lea dreams that the teapot her grandmother gave her is magic.
She believes she has been granted three wishes.

Available August, 2007

Tea With Daddy
Emma Lea prepares a special tea party for her father.
This becomes a memorable tea-for-two afternoon.

Available November, 2007

For more Emma Lea stories, visit our website and online store at www.emmaleabooks.com